THE LITTLE PRINCE

Antoine de Saint-Exupéry, born in Lyon on 29 June 1900, was a French writer and aviator. In 1921, he began his military service and trained as a pilot, and at the outbreak of the Second World War, he joined the French Air Force, flying reconnaissance missions. Later, he joined the Free French Forces, but while flying a mission in Rhone valley on 31 July 1944, he disappeared and was never seen again. It was assumed that he was shot down over the Mediterranean. An unidentifiable body wearing French colours was found several days later and buried in Carqueiranne that September.

THE LITTLE PRINCE

Antoine de Saint-Exupéry

MACMILLAN

First published in 1943 as *Le Petit Prince* by Reynal & Hitchcock, New York
This edition first published 2017 by Macmillan
an imprint of Pan Macmillan Publishing India Private Limited
707, Kailash Building,
26, K. G. Marg, New Delhi – 110 001
www.panmacmillan.co.in

Pan Macmillan, 6 Briset St, Farringdon, London EC1M 5NR
Associated companies throughout the world
www.panmacmillan.com

ISBN 978-93-86215-20-8

5 7 9 8 6 4

Typeset by R. Ajith Kumar, New Delhi
Printed and bound in India by Replika Press Pvt. Ltd.

MIX
Paper | Supporting responsible forestry
FSC www.fsc.org FSC™ C016779

CHAPTER I

I was six years old when I spotted a magnificent picture in a book about an ancient forest. The picture showed a boa constrictor in the act of swallowing a wild beast. This is what it looked like:

It said in the book: 'A boa constrictor swallows its prey whole, without chewing it. After this, it is unable to move and sleeps through the next six months – this is needed for digestion.'

I thought deeply about the experiences of the forest. Then, with care and a coloured pencil, I succeeded in making my first drawing. Drawing Number One looked like this:

I showed my fine work to the grown-ups, and asked if the drawing scared them. 'Scared? Why, it is only a hat!'

But it was not a hat! It was very clearly a boa constrictor digesting an elephant. But the grown-ups need explanations for everything. So, I made another drawing showing the elephant inside the boa constrictor. Drawing Number Two looked like this:

This time, the grown-ups advised me to put away my representations of the boa constrictor, be it from the inside or the outside, and instead spend my time learning geography, history, arithmetic and grammar. That is why at six years of age, I gave up a promising career as an artist, disappointed by the failure of Drawing Number One and Drawing Number Two. Grown-ups find it hard to understand anything on their own, and it is tiring for children to always have to explain things to them.

Hence, I chose a different occupation, and learned to fly airplanes. I flew all over the world and found that geography was very useful to me. I can easily distinguish China from Arizona, and such knowledge is important if you get lost in the dark.

Through the years I have encountered many people of importance and spent a great deal of time among grown-ups. However, knowing them closely hasn't much improved my opinion of them. Whenever I felt I met someone sensible, I experimented by showing him or her my Drawing Number One, which I always carried with me. But, no matter who it was, the answer would always be, 'It is a hat.'

There would end any talk about boa constrictors, or ancient forests, or the stars. I would lower myself to their level and prattle about bridges, and golf, politics, and neckties. Oh how it pleased the grown-ups to have met such a logical man.

CHAPTER 2

So I lived by myself, with no one to talk to, till six years ago, my plane came down in the Sahara Desert with a broken engine. Without a mechanic or any passengers, I ventured to perform the difficult repairs on my own. It was a matter of life and death – there wasn't enough drinking water to last a week.

Miles away from civilization, I spent my first night on the sand, more lost than a castaway in the middle of a vast ocean. So imagine my astonishment when a strange voice woke me the next morning.

It said: 'Please ... could you draw me a sheep!'

'What!'

'Draw me a sheep!'

Utterly startled, I sprang up. Blinking hard, I surveyed the area around myself cautiously. There stood an incredibly small person studying me intently. This is the best portrait I could manage from memory. But the actual person was far more fascinating.

The fault is not mine. Discouraged from becoming a painter when I was six years old, I only know how to draw boas from the inside and from the outside.

Now this sudden vision made my eyes fall out of my head in disbelief. As you are aware, I had crash-landed in

the desert many miles from any habitation. Yet this fellow seemed neither weary nor astray; he wasn't even fainting from hunger or thirst or fear. He did not look like a child lost in the middle of the desert, far away from any living thing. When I finally found I could speak, I asked him, 'What are you doing here?'

'Please … could you draw me a sheep?' he repeated slowly, with care, as if this was a matter of great importance.

So compelling was the situation that I could not disobey. Even though I was far removed from civilization and worried for my life, I took out of my pocket a sheet of paper and my fountain pen. Then it struck me that my studies had been centred around geography, history, arithmetic, and grammar, and I told the little man (with some irritation) that I did not know how to draw.

He answered, 'No matter. Draw me a sheep.'

But I had no experience of drawing a sheep. So I drew for him the thing I so frequently drew – the boa constrictor from the outside. And I was surprised to hear, 'No, no, no! I do not want a boa constrictor with an elephant in its stomach. A boa constrictor is very dangerous and an elephant too bulky. Everything is very small where I come from. A sheep will be more suitable. Draw me a sheep.'

So I made this drawing:

He looked at it carefully and said, 'This won't do. The sheep looks ill. Draw me another.'

I made another drawing:

My friend smiled kindly. 'See for yourself,' he said. 'It is a ram with horns, not a sheep.'

So I made a third drawing:

'It looks ancient!' he exclaimed. I want a sheep that will live for a very long time.'

I was exhausted, and impatient to start working on the crippled engine. So I quickly drew this:

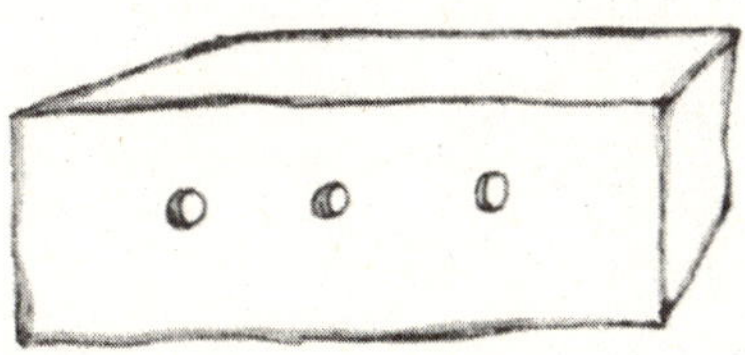

'Your sheep is inside this box,' I explained.

I was pleasantly surprised to see his face light up. 'That is just what I wanted! Do you think this sheep will need plenty of grass?'

'Why?'

'Because my world is very small.'

'Of course there will be enough grass,' I said. 'It is a tiny sheep.'

He bent over the drawing and looked closely. 'Not too tiny ... oh look! He has gone to sleep.'

And that is how I first met the little prince.

CHAPTER 3

It was a long time before I could learn anything about the world he came from. The little prince asked me question after question, but never seemed to hear mine. It was from carelessly dropped words that I gradually constructed the tale.

When he noticed my plane for the first time, for instance (no, I shall not draw it; it is too complicated), he asked me, 'What is that thing?'

'That is not a thing. It can fly. It is a plane. It is *my* airplane.'

I was quite proud to have him know that I was a pilot and could fly the plane.

He cried out, 'Oh my! So you dropped out of the sky?'

'Yes,' I answered, humbly.

'That is so funny!'

And the little prince broke into a ringing laugh, which displeased me very much. I expect others to take my problems seriously.

Then he said, 'So you have come from the sky too! From which planet?'

At that instant I realized he was giving me an important hint about himself, and I said, 'You're from a different planet, aren't you?'

He did not respond. Gazing steadily at my plane he remarked, 'In that thing, you couldn't have come from very far away.'

Then, for what seemed like a long time, he stood lost in thought. Eventually, he took my sheep out of his pocket and looked at it closely.

As you can imagine, I was intrigued when he suggested he was from another planet, so I tried to find out more.

'Where are you from? What is this "small place" you speak of? Where are you going to take my sheep?'

He thought for a while and answered, 'It is good that he has the box. At night, he can use it as his house.'

'Quite right. And if you behave, I can give you a rope to tie him with during the day, and also a post to which he can be tied.'

The little prince was aghast, 'Tie him! Why would we do such a strange thing?'

'But if you don't,' I said, 'will he not wander off and get lost?'

My little friend burst out laughing again.

'But where do you think he would go?'

'Anywhere, I suppose. As his nose guides him.'

He answered solemnly, 'It doesn't matter. In my world, everything is really small!' And then with a touch of sadness, the little prince added:

'Letting his nose guide him will not get him very far.'

CHAPTER 4

I was thus able to learn a second important fact: that the planet the little prince came from was as small as a house!

But I don't know why I was so surprised. I was aware that besides the great planets, the ones we have named Earth, Jupiter, Mars, Venus, there are also many, many others, some of which are so tiny that it is difficult to spot them even through the telescope. When an astronomer discovers a new planet he gives it a number instead of a name. Something like 'Asteroid 325'.

I strongly believe that the little prince's planet is the asteroid known as B-612. This asteroid has only been seen once through a telescope, by a Turkish astronomer, in 1909.

This astronomer presented his discovery at the International Astronomical Congress, but he was completely ignored because of his Turkish dress. Grown-ups can often be like that.

Thankfully for the Asteroid B-612, a Turkish dictator decreed that his subjects must dress in European clothes or face death. So the astronomer made his presentation again in 1920, this time dressed in a handsome suit. He was able to convince everyone.

I have given you these details about the asteroid, because of the grown-ups – they seem to love numbers. When they hear that you have made a new friend, they ask the most unimportant questions. They never say, 'What does his voice sound like? What games does he love best? Does he collect butterflies?' Instead, they ask: 'How old is he? How many brothers has he? What is his weight? Does his father make much money?' From these numbers

alone they think they have learned everything about him. For instance, if you were to say to the grown-ups: 'I saw a beautiful brick house with geraniums in the windows and doves on the roof,' they would be confused. But if you say, 'I saw a house worth a million dollars,' they would remark, 'What a pretty house!'

So, if you say to them, 'The little prince exists! He was so very nice and charming. He laughed and he asked for a sheep. Only a real person wants a sheep,' the grown-ups would only shrug their shoulders and think you were being childish. However, if you were to say, 'He came from Asteroid B-612,' they would be convinced, and would leave you in peace. That is how they are! You must not hold it against them. Children need to be very patient with grown-ups.

For those of us who understand life, numbers are not so critical. If only I could begin this story like a fairy tale.

Then I would say, 'Once upon a time there was a little prince, who lived on a planet barely bigger than himself. He was in search of a friend ...'

I do not want anyone to read my book carelessly. Reliving these memories has made me sad. It has been six years since my friend departed, along with his sheep. I must try to describe him here, to make sure that I don't ever forget him. To forget a friend is terrible. Not everyone has had a friend.

I do not want to be like the grown-ups who are only interested in numbers. So, I have bought a box of paints and some pencils. It is so hard to return to drawing at my age, when all I have ever produced are two pictures of a boa constrictor, from the outside and the inside, at the age of six. I will certainly try to make my portraits as realistic as possible. But I don't know if I will succeed. One drawing looks fine, but the other looks nothing like him. I don't seem to get the little prince's height right either. He is too tall in one and too small in another. Neither am I sure about the colour of his clothes. So I try as best as I can – sometimes getting it right, sometimes not. You must excuse my mistakes. It is not my fault. My friend never gave me any explanations. He thought, perhaps, that I was like him. But, alas, I cannot see sheep through the walls of boxes. Maybe I am a bit like the grown-ups. Maybe I have grown old.

CHAPTER 5

With each passing day I would learn a bit more about the little prince's planet, his departure from it and his journey. The facts came slowly and often unexpectedly. That is how I heard, on the third day, about the baobab crisis.

I had the sheep to thank for it, again. 'Is it true that sheep eat shrubs?' the little prince asked me suddenly.

'Yes, this is true.'

'Oh I am relieved!'

I couldn't understand why it was good that sheep ate shrubs. But the little prince added: 'That would mean they also eat baobabs?'

I explained to him that baobabs were not shrubs but massive trees, as big as castles, and that even if he took along a whole herd of elephants, they could not completely consume one single baobab.

The little prince laughed at the idea of the elephants. 'They would have to be placed one on top of the other,' he said. 'But before the baobabs grow so big, they are quite little,' he commented wisely.

'That is true,' I said. 'But why would you want the sheep to eat the little baobabs?'

'Oh come on!' he said, as if it was the most obvious thing. And I was forced to search my own brain for an answer.

I learned in due course that the little prince's planet, like planets everywhere, had good plants and bad plants. From these came good seeds and bad seeds. But seeds are invisible. They sleep deep in the soil until one among them begins to stir. The little seed stretches itself and cautiously pushes out a harmless little sprig upwards, facing the sun. If it is simply radish or a rose bush, it could be left to grow wherever it might wish. But a bad plant, once it has been identified, must be destroyed at once.

Now, there were some terrible seeds on the little prince's planet – the seeds of the baobab.

The soil of the planet was overrun with them. One could not let these baobabs grow freely. It would take over the entire planet and the roots would burrow their way down. And if it's a small planet the baobabs would wreck it entirely.

'It is all about discipline,' the little prince explained to me. 'When you've finished your washing and cleaning in the morning, it is time to take care of your planet. You must regularly pull out the baobabs the moment you can distinguish them from the rosebushes. The baobabs look just like rose bushes in their youth. It is tiring work, but very easy.'

Then he said to me, 'You must make a beautiful drawing to inform the children on your planet about the baobabs. This would come in handy if they were to travel someday.' He added, 'Sometimes it is all right to put something off for a later day. But baobabs need to be uprooted at once, otherwise they would lead to a disaster. I once knew a layabout who neglected three little bushes on the planet that was his home …'

So, from the description that the little prince provided, I made a drawing of that planet.

I am not trying to preach, but the baobabs are a hazard that is not at all understood; especially those who might get lost on an asteroid must be told about them. Therefore, I quietly did what I was asked. I worked energetically on this drawing so that my friends could be informed of this serious danger. So I say: Children, watch out for the baobabs!

You might find it curious that there is no other drawing in the book as spectacular as that of the baobabs. I did try; I tried very hard, but without any success. With the baobabs, I think, I was compelled by the grave importance of the matter.

CHAPTER 6

Oh, little prince, slowly I begin to piece together the secrets of your sad life. For so long you have found your happiness looking at beautiful sunsets. It was on the fourth morning that I learnt of this fact, when you said to me:

'I do love sunsets. Let us go and watch one now.'

'But we must wait.'

'Wait? For what?'

'Wait until it is time for sunset.'

You seemed puzzled at first. Then you laughed and said: 'I keep forgetting that I'm not at home!'

He had clearly forgotten. It is a known fact that when it is noontime in America, the sun is setting over France. If you could swiftly zip through the air to France, you would be able to watch the sun go down.

Unfortunately, France is too far away. But on your planet, my little prince, all you need to do is revolve your chair a little and watch night fall.

'I watched forty-four sunsets one day!'

'You know,' you added sometime later, 'when people are sad, they watch sunsets.'

'Were you sad too, my little friend,' I asked, 'the day you watched the forty-four sunsets?'

But there was no reply.

CHAPTER 7

The fifth day, thanks to the sheep again, revealed another secret from the little prince's life. Suddenly, surfacing as if from very deep thought, he asked:

'If a sheep eats little bushes, does it eat flowers too?'

'A sheep will eat anything it finds.'

'Even flowers with thorns?'

'Yes, even flowers with thorns.'

'Then what are the thorns for?'

I did not have a clue. I was busy trying to remove a bolt that had lodged itself in the engine. I was really worried. It was becoming clear to me that the damage to my plane was extremely serious. My drinking water was almost exhausted. I feared the worst.

'So what are the thorns for?'

The little prince could never let go of a question, once he had asked it. I, with my mind still on the stubborn bolt, said the first thing that I could think of:

'They are useless. Flowers have thorns because they are cruel!'

'Oh!'

After a moment's silence, the little prince snapped back:

'I don't believe you! Flowers are delicate and faultless. They make up for their innocence with their thorns.'

I did not answer.

At that moment I was thinking: 'If this bolt doesn't turn, I am going to need a hammer.'

Again the little prince interrupted.

'You actually believe that the flowers …'

'No!' I yelled. 'I don't believe anything. Do you not see – I am busy with something important!'

He gaped at me, confused.

'Something important!'

He looked at me stooping over an object that seemed ugly to him, with a hammer in my hand and my fingers black with engine grease.

'You sound exactly like the grown-ups!'

I was a little ashamed when I heard that. He went on, a little harshly:

'And you are wrong! You get everything jumbled up!'

He was really very upset and he tossed his golden hair in the breeze.

'I know of a planet where there's a red-faced man. He has never smelled a flower. He has never looked upon a star. He has never loved anyone. He has done nothing else but sums. And he repeats to himself daily, just like you: "I am busy with something important!" And that makes him swell up with pride. But he is not a man, he is a balloon!'

'A what?'

'A balloon!'

The little prince turned pale with rage.

'Flowers have been growing thorns for millions of years. And for millions of years sheep have been eating them just the same. Is it not important to try and understand why flowers go to so much trouble to grow thorns if they are of no use? The conflict between sheep and flowers is more important than a red-faced man's sums, is it not? What if I told you I know of this one flower that is absolutely unique and can be found only on my planet and at any time it could be bitten off by a sheep? Don't you think that's important?

Red in the face, he continued, 'If you love a flower which is one of its kind on the millions of stars in the sky, it is enough to just look at the stars and feel happy. You can say to yourself, "I know my flower is out there somewhere." But if a sheep eats the flower, all the stars will seem to darken. How can you not think that is important!'

He burst into tears and stopped talking. The day had turned to night and I let my tools drop.

My concerns too fell away – the hammer, the bolt, my thirst and the thoughts of dying. There was a star, a planet, my own planet Earth and a little prince who needed to be consoled. I held him in my arms and said to him:

'The flower you love is in no danger at all. I will draw a muzzle for your sheep and a mesh to protect your flower. I will ...' I did not know how to continue. I felt like a fool. I did not know how to help him. The world of tears is such a mystery.

CHAPTER 8

I soon learned more about the flower. Flowers were simple things on the little prince's planet and took up very little room. They only had a single ring of petals and were not at all demanding. They would appear in the grass one morning and fade away peacefully by evening. But one day, a seed that had blown in from some other place, gave birth to a new type of shoot and the little prince watched over it very closely. What if it was some new kind of baobab! But the shrub soon stopped growing, and began to produce a flower. At the first appearance of a huge bud, the little prince felt he was in the presence of a miracle. But the flower took her time in its green sacntuary, getting ready to emerge. She chose her colours thoughtfully. She adjusted her petals one by one. After all, she did not wish to appear crumpled like a poppy. She wished to materialize in all her beauty. Oh was she proud! And these secret preparations lasted for many days. Then at sunrise one morning, she showed herself.

She yawned and said: 'I am barely awake. Forgive me, my petals are such a mess.'

But the little prince was full of admiration: 'Oh! How beautiful you are!'

'Am I not?' the flower responded sweetly. 'And I was born along with the sun.'

The little prince could tell that she wasn't exactly humble. But she was just so wonderful!

'Is it not time for breakfast?' she asked a moment later. 'If you would kindly think of my needs …' Feeling embarrassed, the little prince went to look for a sprinkling can and gave her some fresh, cool water.

Very soon, she began to trouble him with her rather thorny pride. For instance, while speaking of her four thorns, she said to the little prince: 'Let the tigers show their claws!'

'We have no tigers on this planet,' the little prince pointed out. 'And, anyway, tigers do not eat weeds.'

'I am not a weed,' was the flower's gentle reply.

'I'm sorry.'

'I am not at all afraid of tigers,' she went on, 'but I am horrified of gales. Would you have a screen for me?'

'Horrified of gales! That's not good luck for a plant,' the little prince thought to himself. 'This flower is a complicated creature.'

'You need to place me under a dome at night. This planet is cold. Where I come from …'

She stopped mid-sentence. She had come from a seed and could not have known about any other world. Embarrassed that her little lie had been exposed, she coughed a few times, to make the little prince feel bad for her. 'What happened to the screen?'

'I was going to look for it but you were still speaking to me!'

Then she forced another cough, so as to make him feel sorry.

So, even though the little prince loved her and would do anything for her, he was now wary of her. Her harsh words had upset him and he felt miserable.

'I shouldn't have paid any heed to her words,' he confided to me. 'You mustn't listen to flowers. You

should simply admire them and enjoy their fragrance. My flower sweetened my planet with her scent, but I could find no pleasure in it. Her chatter about the claws, that so irritated me, should have made me feel bad for her instead.'

He continued: 'I made a mistake! I should have judged her by her deeds and not by her words. She filled my world with light and her perfume. I should not have run away. I should have noticed that she cared underneath all her games. Flowers are incomprehensible! Or maybe I wasn't old enough to know how to love her.'

CHAPTER 9

I believe the little prince escaped with the help of a flight of migratory birds.

On the morning of his departure he made sure his planet was in perfect order. He carefully cleaned out the active volcanoes. The two active volcanoes on the planet were just right for making his breakfast in the morning. He also cleaned the only extinct volcano because, as he said, 'One never knows!'

When cleaned well, volcanoes burn slowly and steadily, without erupting. Volcanic eruptions are like fires in a chimney. Here on earth we are much too small to clean out our volcanoes. That is why they bring all this trouble upon us.

The little prince also pulled up the last of the baobab shoots, feeling a little sad as he did so. He believed that he would not return. But on this morning, all his familiar tasks seemed most delightful. And when he watered the flower for the last time, getting ready to place her under her dome, he realized that he was very close to tears.

'Goodbye,' he said to the flower.

But there came no answer.

'Goodbye,' he repeated.

The flower coughed, not because she had a cold.

'I have been rather silly,' she said to him at last. 'Do forgive me, and try to be happy.'

He was surprised that she wasn't complaining. He stood, holding the glass dome in the air. He did not understand this sudden tenderness.

'I love you, this is true,' the flower said to him. 'It is my fault I did not make this clear to you. But you have been as foolish as me. Try to be happy. Let the dome be. I don't want it anymore.'

'But the gales …'

'My cold is not that serious. The cool night air is good for me. I am a flower.'

'And the beasts …'

'Well, I should endure two or three caterpillars if I wish to meet the butterflies. They are very beautiful, I've heard. If not the butterflies and the caterpillars, who would come to see me? You will be somewhere far. As for the wild animals, they don't scare me. I have my thorns.'

Saying this, she revealed her four thorns.

'Don't linger on. You are annoying me. You have decided to leave, so leave!'

She did not wish for him to see her tears, the proud flower that she was.

The little prince resumed cleaning the active volcano.

CHAPTER 10

The little prince found himself close to the asteroids 325, 326, 327, 328, 329 and 330. He started visiting them one by one, so he would have something to do as well as be able to learn about the universe.

The first asteroid was inhabited by a king. Clad in royal purple and ermine, he sat upon a throne that was both simple and regal.

'Ah! A subject,' exclaimed the king, when he saw the little prince approach.

'But how could he know me? He has never met me before,' thought the little prince.

He did not yet know how simple things were for kings. To them, everyone is a subject.

'Come closer, so that I may see you better,' said the king, feeling glad that he could finally rule over someone.

The little prince looked around to find something to sit on, but the planet was completely covered by the king's magnificent robe.

So he remained standing and since he was tired, he started to yawn.

'It is not polite to yawn in the presence of a king,' said the emperor. 'I forbid you to do so.'

'I can't help myself,' replied the little prince, red-faced. 'I have come a long way, and I have had no sleep.'

'Then I command you to yawn,' the king said. 'I have not witnessed a yawn in years. I find yawns rather interesting. Go on, yawn for me – it is an order.

'I … I am feeling shy,' murmured the little prince.

'Hmm!' replied the king. 'Then I … I order you to sometimes yawn and sometimes not …' He paused, looking a little uncertain.

What the king really wanted was respect for his authority. He did not wish for any disobedience. He was an emperor through and through. But, he was also a kind man, so his orders were always reasonable.

'If I demand that a general,' he would frequently say, 'should transform into a sea bird and if the general is unable to do so, that would not be his fault. It would be mine.'

'May I sit down?' the little prince enquired timidly.

'I command you to sit,' the king answered, and majestically gathered in a fold of his ermine robe to make room.

The little prince was wondering: the planet was really small … what was it that the king reigned over?

'Your Majesty,' he said to the king, 'could I ask you a question …'

'I command you to ask me a question,' the king hastily replied.

'Sire, over what do you rule?'

'Over everything,' said the king, with great simplicity.

'Over everything?'

With a sweeping gesture, the king indicated his planet, the other planets, and all the stars.

'Over all that?' asked the little prince.

'Over all that,' the king answered.

After all, his rule was not only absolute, it was also universal.

'And do the stars obey you?'

'Certainly they do,' the king said. 'They obey instantly. I do not permit wild behaviour.'

The little prince marvelled at such power. If he wielded such authority, he would not watch only forty-four sunsets a day, but seventy-two or a hundred, or even two hundred, without ever having to move his chair! Feeling a little homesick, as he remembered the planet he had forsaken, he dared to ask the king for a favour:

'I would love to see a sunset. Could you order the sun to set ... for me?'

'If I commanded a general to dart from flower to flower like a butterfly, or to write a tragedy, or to turn into a sea bird, and if the general defied the order, who would be in the wrong?' the king demanded. 'Him or myself?'

'You,' the little prince said firmly.

'That is right. One must demand what can be given,' the king went on. 'Authority basically rests on reason. If you commanded your subjects to throw themselves into the sea, they would mutiny. I demand obedience because my orders are reasonable.'

'But, what about my sunset?' the little prince reminded him. He could never let a question be.

'You shall have your sunset. I shall command it. But, I will await the right conditions.'

'When would that be?' inquired the little prince.

'Hmm!' replied the king, carefully examining a massive calendar. 'Hmm! Hmm! That will be at about ... about ... twenty minutes to eight this evening. And you will see then how well my commands are obeyed.'

The little prince yawned. He was unhappy to have foregone his sunset. And he was also a little bored. 'There's nothing else for me to do here,' he said to the king. 'I'm going to continue on my travels now.'

'You can't leave,' said the king, who was very proud to have a subject. 'You must not leave. I will make you a minister!'

'Minister of what?'

'Minster of ... of justice!'

'But there is no one here I could judge!'

'How could we know?' the king said to him. 'I have not yet surveyed the whole kingdom. I am very old. There is no room here for a carriage. And walking tires me easily.'

'Oh, but I have looked already,' said the little prince, turning around to give all sides of the planet another glance. 'There is no one anywhere.'

'Then you must judge yourself,' said the king. 'It is the hardest thing to do. It is much more difficult to judge oneself than to judge others. But if you succeed, then you are indeed a wise man.'

'Yes,' said the little prince, 'but to judge myself I do not need to live here. I can do it anywhere.'

'Hmm!' said the king. 'I believe that somewhere on my planet there is an old rat. I can hear him at night. You could judge him. From time to time you will condemn him to death, so that his life will depend on your justice. But you must forgive him each time and so spare his life. He is the only rat we have.'

'I wouldn't like to condemn anyone to death,' said the little prince. 'I think I shall be off now.'

'No,' said the king.

But the little prince was all set to depart, though he did not wish to hurt the old monarch.

'If Your Majesty wishes to be obeyed,' he said, 'he could give me a reasonable order. He could, for example, command me to be gone within a minute. The conditions seem quite favourable.'

The king gave no answer. The little prince hesitated for a second, then, with a sigh, he got up to leave.

'I will make you my ambassador!' the king called out in haste.

He exuded such authority.

'Grown-ups really are peculiar,' the little prince said to himself, as he resumed his journey.

CHAPTER 11

On the second planet lived a show-off.

'Aha! I see an admirer!' he declared from afar, as soon as he spotted the little prince.

For a show-off, everyone is an admirer.

'Hello,' said the little prince. 'What an odd hat!'

'It is a hat I raise as I bow,' the show-off replied. 'I raise it when I am praised. Unfortunately, nobody ever goes through here.'

'Oh?' said the confused little prince.

'Clap your hands,' the show-off said to him. When the little prince did so, the show-off raised his hat in a modest salute.

'This is much more amusing than the visit to the king,' the little prince said to himself. And he began to clap his hands again. The show-off raised his hat in acknowledgement.

After five minutes of this exercise, the little prince grew weary.

'And what should I do to drop your hat to the floor?' he asked.

But the show-off did not hear him. Show-offs are deaf to everything but praise.

'Do you really find me very admirable?' he asked the little prince.

'What do you mean by "admirable"?'

'It means you regard me as the handsomest, smartest, richest, and wisest man on this planet.'

'But you are the only one on this planet!'

'Nevertheless, admire me so I may feel happy.'

'I admire you,' said the little prince, shrugging his shoulders slightly, 'but why does this matter to you so much?'

Saying this, the little prince went away.

'Grown-ups really are peculiar,' he said to himself, as he continued on his way.

CHAPTER 12

On the third planet lived a drunkard. The little prince's visit here was brief, and it left him feeling rather sad.

'What are you doing?' he asked the drunkard, who sat quietly before an assortment of bottles, some full, some empty.

'I am drinking,' the drunkard replied.

'Why are you drinking?' the little prince wanted to know.

'To forget,' replied the drunkard.

'Forget what?' inquired the little prince, who was already feeling sorry for him.

'Forget that I am ashamed,' the drunkard confessed, hanging his head.

'What are you ashamed of?' insisted the little prince, who wanted to help him.

'Ashamed of drinking!' said the drunkard and then he was absolutely silent.

The little prince went away, feeling rather confused.

'Grown-ups really are peculiar,' he said to himself, as he resumed his travels.

CHAPTER 13

The fourth planet belonged to a businessman. This man was so preoccupied that he did not even look up when the little prince arrived.

'Hello there,' the little prince said. 'Your cigarette's out.'

'Three plus two is five. Five and seven make twelve. Twelve and three make fifteen. Oh hello! Fifteen plus seven is twenty-two. Twenty-two and six make twenty-eight. I do not have time to light it again. Twenty-six and five make thirty-one. Whew! That comes to five-hundred-and-one-million, six-hundred-twenty-two-thousand, seven-hundred-thirty-one.'

'Five hundred million what?'

'Eh? You are still here? Five hundred and one million ... what was it ... I have so much to do! I am very busy with important matters. I have no time to waste. Two and five make seven ...'

'Five hundred and one million what?' repeated the little prince, who could never let go of a question.

The businessman looked up. 'In all the fifty-four years I have spent on this planet, I have been interrupted only thrice. The first time was twenty-two years ago by an irate hornet, from goodness knows where – it made the most

frightful racket and I made four mistakes in my sums. The second time was eleven years ago, when I suffered an attack of rheumatism. I don't get enough exercise. I have no time to be lazy either. I have too many important things to do. The third time is, well, now! Five hundred and one million …'

'Million what?'

The businessman finally realized that there was no way he could avoid the question.

'Millions of those little objects in the sky.'

'Flies?'

'Oh no! The shiny ones.'

'Are you talking about bees?'

'No, no. The little golden objects that cause people to daydream. As for me, I have no time for that. I deal in matters of consequence.'

'You mean the stars?'

'Yes, the stars.'

'And what will you do with five hundred million stars?'

'Five hundred and one million, six hundred and twenty-two thousand, seven hundred and thirty-one. I am concerned with serious matters. I am always exact.'

'And what do you do with these stars?'

'What do I do with them?'

'Yes.'

'Nothing. I own them.'

'You own the stars?'

'Yes.'

'But I met a king who …'

'Kings do not own, they "rule". It's altogether different.'

'And what good does it do to own stars?'

'It makes me rich.'

'And how does it help being rich?'

'I can buy more stars, if any more are discovered.'

'This man,' the little prince said to himself, 'argues like the drunkard …'

He continued to ask more questions. 'How is it possible to own the stars?'

'Who do they belong to?' the businessman retorted, irritably.

'I don't know. To nobody.'

'Then they belong to me. I was the first person to think of it.'

'Is that it?'

'Certainly. When you find a diamond that nobody claims, it becomes yours.

When you discover an island that belongs to nobody, it is yours. When an idea comes to you before it does to anyone else, you put a patent on it: it too is yours. So, I own the stars because nobody else thought of owning them.'

'Yes, I suppose that's true,' said the little prince. 'And what do you do with the stars?'

'I oversee them,' replied the businessman. 'I count and recount them. It isn't easy work, but I am diligent.'

The little prince was not satisfied.

'If I have a scarf,' he said, 'I could wrap it around my neck and take it with me. If I have a flower, I could pluck that flower and take it with me. But you cannot pluck the stars.'

'No. But I can put them in the bank.'

'Whatever do you mean?'

'What it means is that, I write the number of my stars on a little piece of paper and then I put this paper in a drawer and lock it with a key.'

'And that is all?'

'That is enough,' said the businessman.

'This is entertaining,' thought the little prince. 'It is rather poetic in fact. But it's of no great consequence.'

On important matters, the little prince's ideas were completely different from those of the grown-ups.

'I own a flower,' he continued, 'that I water every day. I own three volcanoes, which I clean out every week. I also clean out the extinct one because one never knows. It is of some use to my volcanoes and to my flower that I own them. But you are of no use to the stars.'

The businessman opened his mouth, but there came no answer.

So the little prince went away.

'Grown-ups are quite astonishing,' he said to himself as he continued on his travels.

CHAPTER 14

The fifth planet was unusual. It was the smallest of them all. There was only enough room on it for a street lamp and a lamplighter. The little prince could not gauge the use of a street lamp and a lamplighter on a planet without people or houses. Still, he thought, 'It may be that this man is absurd. But he is not as absurd as the king, the show-off, the businessman, or the drunkard. At least his work has some meaning. When he lights his street lamp, it is like he's brought another star to life, or a flower. When he puts it out, he puts the star or the flower to sleep. It's a wonderful job. And so it is truly useful.'

When he arrived on the planet he politely said to the lamplighter:

'Hello! Why have you put your lamp out?'

'Those are my orders,' replied the lamplighter. 'Hello.'

'What exactly are your orders?'

'That I put out my lamp. Goodnight.'

And he lit his lamp again.

'But why did you light it again?'

'Those are my orders,' said the lamplighter.

'I can't understand,' said the little prince.

'There is nothing to understand,' said the lamplighter.

'Orders are orders. Good morning.'

And he put out his lamp.

Then he mopped his forehead with a red checkered handkerchief.

'Mine is a tough job. It wasn't so before. I would put the lamp out in the morning and light it in the evening. I had the rest of the day to relax and the night for sleeping.'

'And have the orders changed since then?'

'The orders have not changed,' said the lamplighter. 'That is the problem! The planet turns faster and faster every year but my orders remain the same!'

'What then?' asked the little prince.

'The planet now revolves once every minute, and I have no time to rest. So every minute I have to light my lamp and then put it out!'

'That is so amusing – a day lasts only a minute here!'

'It is not amusing at all!' said the lamplighter. 'We have been talking for a month already.'

'A month?'

'Yes. Thirty minutes equals thirty days! Goodnight.'

And he lighted his lamp again.

The little prince watched him. He really liked this lamplighter who was so faithful to his orders. He remembered the sunsets on his own planet. He could watch them by simply moving his chair. He wanted to help his friend. 'You know,' he said, 'I can show you a way to rest whenever you want to.'

'I want to rest all the time,' said the lamplighter.

It is possible for a person to be faithful and lazy at the same time.

The little prince explained: 'Your planet is very small. It takes only three strides to go around it. To be in the light, you need to walk slowly. When you want to rest, you walk … and the day will last as long as you like.'

'That doesn't do me any good,' said the lamplighter. 'What I like to do is sleep.'

'That's unlucky,' said the little prince.

'It is unlucky,' said the lamplighter. 'Hello.'

And he put out his lamp.

'That man,' said the little prince to himself, as he continued on his journey, 'would be scorned by the king, the show-off, the drunkard and the businessman. Yet he is the only one who does not seem ridiculous to me. Perhaps, it is because he cares for something besides himself.'

He breathed a sigh of regret, and thought, 'That man is the only one who could have been my friend. But his planet is just too small and wouldn't have room for two people.'

What the little prince wouldn't admit to himself was that the most exciting aspect of the planet was its fourteen hundred and forty sunsets, every twenty-four hours!

CHAPTER 15

The sixth planet was ten times bigger than the last. There lived an elderly gentleman who wrote long books.

'Ah! Here comes an explorer!' he exclaimed when he saw the little prince.

The little prince rested on a table to catch his breath. He had been travelling for so long!

'Where do you come from?' the old gentleman asked.

'What is that big book?' said the little prince. 'What are you doing?'

'I am a geographer,' the old gentleman said to him.

'What is a geographer?' asked the little prince.

'A geographer is a scholar who knows the location of the seas, rivers, towns, mountains, and deserts.'

'That is quite interesting,' said the little prince. 'Here at last is a man with a real job!' And he cast a look around the planet. It was the most spectacular planet he had ever seen.

'Your planet is very beautiful,' he said. 'Does it have oceans?'

'I wouldn't know,' said the geographer.

'Oh!' The little prince was disappointed. 'What about mountains?'

'I couldn't say,' said the geographer.

'How about cities and rivers and deserts?'

'I don't know that either.'

'But you are a geographer!'

'That I am,' the geographer admitted. 'But I am no explorer! I don't have a single explorer on my planet. A geographer is much too important to go around and count the towns, rivers, mountains, seas, oceans and deserts. He does not leave his desk. He receives the explorers in his study and asks them questions. Then he notes down what they remember of their travels. And if any account interests him, the geographer has the explorer's moral character verified.'

'Why is that?'

'Because a lying explorer would be disastrous for the geography books. As would an explorer who drank too much.'

'Why is that?' asked the little prince.

'Because drunkards see double. And the geographer would note down two mountains where there should only be one.'

'I know a person,' said the little prince, 'who would make a bad explorer.'

'That is possible. Then, when the moral character of the explorer is verified, an inquiry is ordered into his discovery.'

'You go and have a look at it?'

'No. That would be too complicated. The explorer must furnish proof. For example, if the discovery is a large mountain, he needs to bring back large rocks.'

The geographer was suddenly excited.

'But you … you come from far away! You are an explorer! You must describe your planet to me!'

The geographer opened his large notebook and sharpened his pencil. All explorer accounts are written in pencil before they are verified. Once evidence is furnished, these accounts are put down in ink.

'Well?' said the geographer expectantly.

'Where I come from,' said the little prince, 'it is not very interesting. My planet is very small. There are three volcanoes – two are active and the other is extinct. But one never knows.'

'One never knows,' repeated the geographer.

'There is a flower too.'

'We do not record flowers,' said the geographer.

'Why don't you? The flower is the most beautiful thing on my planet!'

'We do not record them,' said the geographer, 'because they are ephemeral.'

'What does "ephemeral" mean?'

'Geography books,' said the geographer, 'are serious books. They never go out of date. It is not very often that a mountain moves or the ocean dries up. We write of everlasting facts.'

'But extinct volcanoes may come to life again,' the little prince interrupted. 'And what does "ephemeral" mean?'

'It doesn't matter to us if volcanoes are extinct or live,' said the geographer. 'What matters to us is the mountain. It does not change.'

'But what does "ephemeral" mean?' repeated the little prince, who would never let go of a question till he got an answer.

'It means "that which will die".'

'Will my flower die?'

'Certainly it will.'

'My flower is ephemeral,' the little prince said to himself, 'and she has only four thorns with which to defend herself against the world. And I have left her all alone!'

This is when he felt the first stab of regret. But he tried to be cheerful.

'Which planet would you advise me to visit?' he asked.

'The planet Earth,' replied the geographer. 'We have heard good things about it.'

And the little prince went away, thinking of his flower.

CHAPTER 16

So the seventh planet was Earth.

The Earth is no ordinary planet! There are one hundred and eleven kings (counting the African kings too), seven thousand geographers, nine hundred thousand businessmen, seven and a half million drunkards as well as three hundred and eleven million show-offs. That comes to around two billion grown-ups.

To give you an idea of the size of the Earth, I must tell you that before the invention of electricity, there were four hundred and sixty-two thousand, five hundred and eleven lamplighters across six continents.

Seen from afar, it was a splendid sight. The movement of this army was regulated like those of the ballet. First in line were the lamplighters of New Zealand and Australia. Having set their lamps alight, they would go off to sleep. The lamplighters of China and Siberia were next, until they moved back into the wings. Then came the lamplighters of Russia and India, followed by those from Africa and Europe. Then came South America, and finally North America. They never made a mistake in the order of their appearance. It was incredible.

Only the lamplighters of the North Pole and the South Pole led carefree lives; they worked only twice a year.

CHAPTER 17

Sometimes people lie to sound smart.

I wasn't being completely honest about the lamplighters. For those who do not know of our planet, it is the wrong picture. People occupy very little space on the Earth. If the two billion inhabitants were placed together, they would quite easily fit into a public square twenty miles long and twenty miles wide. All humanity could be piled up on a small Pacific island.

The grown-ups will not believe you. They feel that they take up a great deal of space. They think they are as large as baobabs. You could ask them to do their own calculations – you know how they adore figures. But do not waste your time on this task – it is of no use, trust me.

When the little prince arrived on Earth, he was surprised not to see any people. He was beginning to worry that he had come to the wrong planet, when a coil the colour of the moon flashed across the sand.

'Good evening,' said the little prince, just in case.

'Good evening,' said the snake.

'What planet is this?' asked the little prince.

'Earth. And we are in Africa,' the snake answered.

'But aren't there any people on Earth?'

'This is a desert. There are no people in the desert. The Earth is huge,' said the snake.

The little prince sat on a rock and looked up at the sky.

'I wonder,' he said, 'whether the stars are lit up so that one day each one of us may find his own star. Look, there's my planet, right there above us. But how far away it is!'

'It is beautiful,' the snake said. 'Why are you here?'

'I have been having some trouble with a flower,' said the little prince.

'Ah!' said the snake. And they were both silent.

'Where are the people?' the little prince said, picking up the conversation again. 'It is a bit lonely in the desert.'

'It is also lonely among men,' the snake said.

The little prince gazed at him for a long time.

'You are funny,' he said at last. 'You are no thicker than a finger …'

'But I am more powerful than the finger of a king,' said the snake.

The little prince smiled. 'No, you are not. You don't even have feet. You cannot even travel …'

'I can carry you farther than any ship,' said the snake.

And saying this, he twined himself around the little prince's ankle, like a golden bracelet.

'Whoever I touch I send back to the dust that created them,' the snake spoke again. 'But you are pure and you come from a star.'

The little prince made no reply.

'I am concerned about you … you are so helpless on this cruel Earth,' the snake said. 'I can help you, someday, if you grow too homesick for your own planet. I can …'

'Oh! I understand what you mean,' said the little prince. 'But why do you always speak in riddles?'

'And I solve them all,' said the snake. With this, they both fell silent.

CHAPTER 18

The little prince walked across the desert to only meet a plant – a flower with three petals.

'Hello,' said the little prince.

'Greetings,' said the flower.

'Where are all the people?' the little prince asked politely.

The flower had once seen a caravan go past.

'People?' she echoed. 'I think there are about six or seven of them. I saw them many years ago. But no one knows where to find them. They are blown about by the winds. They have no roots, and this causes them many problems.'

'Goodbye,' said the little prince.

'Goodbye,' said the flower.

CHAPTER 19

The little prince climbed to the top of a high mountain. The three volcanoes on his planet were the only mountains he had ever known, and they were only as high as his knees. He used the extinct volcano as a stool. 'From a

mountain as high as this,' he said to himself, 'I will be able to see the whole planet and all its people at once.' But he saw nothing but sharp, craggy peaks.

'Hello,' he said, just in case.

'Hello … hello … hello,' answered the echo.

'Who are you?' said the little prince.

'Who are you … who are you … who are you?' answered the echo.

'I need some friends – I am all alone,' he said.

'All alone … all alone … all alone,' answered the echo.

'What a peculiar planet!' thought the little prince. 'It is too dry, too pointed, and salty. And the people seem to have no imagination. They repeat whatever is said to them … On my planet I had a flower, and she was always the first to speak.'

CHAPTER 20

After walking for a very long time through sand, rocks and snow, the little prince at last came upon a road. And all roads ultimately lead to people.

So he said, 'Hello.'

He was standing before a garden of roses in full bloom.

'Hello,' said the roses.

The little prince stared at the roses. They looked just like his flower.

'Who are you?' he asked in wonderment.

'We are roses,' the roses said.

The little prince was overcome with sadness. His flower had said that she was one of a kind in all the universe. And here were five thousand of them, all alike, in a single garden!

'She would be very upset,' he said to himself, 'if she came to this garden. She would cough most dreadfully, and pretend that she was dying just to avoid looking like a fool. And I would have to pretend to take care of her, for if I did not, she would surely allow herself to die, just to make me feel bad.'

'I thought that I was lucky,' the little prince said to himself, 'that I had a flower so unique. But all I had was a common rose. A common rose and three small volcanoes, of which one might be extinct. That doesn't really make me a prince.'

And he lay down on the grass and cried.

CHAPTER 21

At that moment the fox appeared.

'Hello,' said the fox.

'Hello,' said the little prince gently, although when he turned around he saw nothing.

'I am here,' the voice said, 'under the apple tree.'

'Who are you?' asked the little prince. 'You are very pretty,' he added.

'I am a fox,' said the fox.

'Come and play with me,' offered the little prince. 'I am so unhappy.'

'I cannot play with you,' the fox said. 'I am not tame.'

'Oh! I'm sorry,' said the little prince. But, after some thought, he added: 'What does "tame" mean?'

'You don't live here,' said the fox. 'What are you searching for?'

'I am searching for people,' said the little prince. 'What does "tame" mean?'

'People!' said the fox. 'They have guns, and they hunt. It is quite a problem. They also breed chickens. That's what they are interested in. Are you looking for chickens?'

'No,' said the little prince. 'I am looking for friends. What does "tame" mean?'

'It is something no one really thinks about,' said the fox. 'It means "to make a connection".'

'Make a connection?'

'Correct,' said the fox. 'For me you are a little boy just like a hundred thousand other little boys. To you I am a fox like a hundred thousand other foxes. We have no need of each other. But, if you were to tame me, then we would need each other. You would be unique to me, and I to you.'

'I am beginning to understand,' said the little prince. 'There's this flower … I think she has tamed me.'

'It is possible,' said the fox. 'Here on Earth one sees all kinds of things.'

'Oh, but it's not on Earth!' said the little prince.

The fox was very curious.

'On another planet?'

'Yes.'

'Are there hunters on this planet?'

'No.'

'How intriguing! Are there any chickens?'

'No.'

'No place is perfect,' sighed the fox.

'My life is so dull,' the fox continued. 'I hunt chickens; men hunt me. All the chickens are identical. All the men are identical. As a result I'm thoroughly bored. But if you tame me, my life will light up. I'll recognize your footsteps from all the others. While other's footfalls drive me underground, yours will draw me out like music. Look there! Do you see the wheat fields? I do not eat bread. Wheat is of no use to me. They remind me of nothing. And that is sad. But your hair is the colour of gold. Imagine how it will be when you have tamed me! I will see the golden wheat and think of you. And the wind whispering through the wheat stalks will make me happy.'

The fox paused and looked longingly at the little prince.

'Please … tame me!' he said.

'I would really like to,' the little prince replied. 'But I have very little time. I have to look for friends and there is still so much to understand.'

'You will understand what you tame,' said the fox. 'People have no time to understand anything anymore. They buy things readymade at the shops. But there is no store where you can buy friendship, and so, people have no friends anymore. If you are looking for a friend, you could tame me.'

'What would I need to do?' asked the little prince.

'You have to be very patient,' replied the fox. 'First, sit some distance away from me on the grass. I will look at you out of the corner of my eye, and you will be quiet. Words can cause misunderstandings. But each day you should come a little closer.'

The next day when the little prince returned, 'You must come back at the same hour every day,' said the fox. 'If, for example, you decide to come at four o'clock in the afternoon, from three o'clock I will begin to feel happy. I will feel happier and happier as the hour advances. At four o'clock, I will start getting agitated. This way I will learn the price of happiness! But if you come at any odd time, I will never know when to be glad … We must have rituals.'

'What is a ritual?' asked the little prince.

'It is also something no one really thinks about,' said the fox. 'Rituals make one day different from the other days, or one hour from the other. My hunters have a ritual. Every Thursday they dance with the village girls. So Thursday is the perfect day for me! I can take a walk right up to the vineyards. But if the hunters danced at any odd time, every day would be the same, and I would never get a day off.'

*

So the little prince tamed the fox. And when it was time for him to depart, 'I am going to cry,' said the fox.

'The fault is your own,' said the little prince. 'I wished you no unhappiness, but you insisted that I tame you.'

'Yes,' said the fox.

'But now you are going to cry!' said the little prince.

'Yes,' said the fox.

'So, it has done you no good!'

'It has done me good — I can now appreciate the colour of the wheat fields.'

Then he added, 'Go and look at the roses again. And it will be clear to you that yours is unique. Then come back to say goodbye to me, and I will give you for a gift a secret.'

*

The little prince left to look at the roses again.

'You are not like my rose at all,' he said to them. 'You are not special yet. No one has tamed you, and you have tamed no one. My fox was like you. He was like a hundred thousand other foxes. But I have made him my friend, and now he is unique.'

And the roses felt quite uneasy.

'You are beautiful, but you are hollow,' he went on. 'No one would give up their life for you. Of course an ordinary passerby would think that my rose looks just like you. But she's more important than all of you – because I watered her, I sheltered her under a glass dome, and I protected her with a mesh. It was for her that I killed the caterpillars (except the two or three so she could see the butterflies). I have listened to her complaining, grumbling, boasting and even to her silence. Because she is *my* rose.'

*

And he went back to see the fox. 'Goodbye,' he said.

'Goodbye,' said the fox. 'Here is my secret, it's a simple secret: it is only through your heart that you can see clearly. The eyes do not see that which is most important.'

'The eyes do not see that which is most important,' the little prince repeated, so that he would remember.

'It is the time you have spent with your rose that makes your rose so important.'

'It is the time I have spent with my rose ...' repeated the little prince, so that he wouldn't forget.

'People ignore this simple truth,' said the fox. 'But you must not. You are forever responsible for those you have tamed. You are responsible for your rose.'

'I am responsible for my rose ...' the little prince repeated, so that he would remember.

CHAPTER 22

'Hello there,' said the little prince.

'Hello,' said the railway signalman.

'What do you do?' the little prince asked.

'I sort travellers into groups of a thousand,' said the signalman. 'Then I send the trains carrying them either to the right or to the left.'

Just then a brightly lit express train thundered by, making the signal box shake.

'Why are they in such a great hurry?' asked the little prince.

'Even the travellers don't know why,' said the signalman.

A second express train roared by, in the opposite direction.

'Are they back already?' the little prince wanted to know.

'They are not the same lot,' said the signalman. 'It is an exchange.'

'Were they unhappy where they were?' asked the little prince.

'Nobody is really happy where they are,' said the signalman.

Now a third express train bellowed past.

'Are they following the first group of travellers?' said the little prince.

'They are following nothing,' said the signalman. 'They are fast asleep in there, or they may be yawning. Only the children press their faces against the windows.'

'Only children know what they are looking for,' said the little prince. 'They amuse themselves with a rag doll for hours and it becomes really important to them. If someone takes it away from them, they cry.'

'Aren't they lucky,' said the signalman.

CHAPTER 23

'Hello,' said the little prince.

'Hello,' said the merchant.

This merchant sold smart little pills that could quench one's thirst.

You consume one pill a week, and you would feel no need to drink anything at all.

'Why do you sell these?' asked the little prince.

'They help save a lot of time,' said the merchant. 'The experts have calculated that you can save fifty-three minutes every week.'

'And what would you do with those fifty-three minutes?'

'Whatever you like.'

'Hmm,' said the little prince to himself. 'If I had fifty-three extra minutes, I would take a stroll to the water fountain.'

CHAPTER 24

It was now the eighth day since my crash in the desert, and I listened to the story of the merchant as I finished the last of my water supply. 'Just a minute now,' I said to the little prince, 'your stories are all great, but I have not repaired my plane yet; I don't have any water, and I too would love to take a walk to the water fountain!'

'My friend the fox …' the little prince began.

'My dear little man, I don't want to know any more about the fox!'

'Why not?'

'Because we are about to die of thirst.'

He could not understand what I was saying. He replied, 'It is always good to have had a friend, even if you are about to die. I am glad that I had a fox as a friend …'

'He doesn't seem to realize the danger,' I said to myself. 'He doesn't feel either hunger or thirst. All he needs is a little sunshine.'

But the little prince looked at me, as if he had heard my thought, 'I am thirsty, too. Let's look for a well.'

I wasn't too enthusiastic, it is ridiculous to look for a well in the desert. But we set out anyway.

As we trudged along for hours, in silence, the stars began to come out in the night sky. Thirst had made me a little feverish, and I saw them as if in a dream. The little prince's last words came drifting back to me.

'You are thirsty, too?' I wanted to know.

But he did not reply. He merely said to me:

'Water is good for the heart, you know.' I did not understand, but I said nothing. I knew how confusing it is to question him. He was tired. He sat down. I sat down next to him. After a while he said, 'The stars are lovely – because of a flower we cannot see.'

'Yes,' I said, and quietly looked out over the ridges of sand that were stretched out before us in the moonlight.

'The desert is beautiful,' the little prince added.

And that was the truth. I have always loved the desert. You may sit down on a sand dune but you will see or hear nothing. Yet, there is something that glows in the silence.

'What makes the desert so beautiful,' said the little prince, 'is that somewhere in its folds lies hidden a well.'

I was surprised as a sudden understanding dawned on me – about the sand's mysterious glow.

I grew up in an old house. It was said that a treasure was hidden there. I don't think anyone had ever known how to find it, or had even looked for it. But it cast a spell over the house – it hid a secret in its depths.

'Yes,' I said to the little prince. 'Be it a house, the stars, the desert – what makes them beautiful stays invisible!'

'I am glad,' he said, 'that you agree with my fox.'

As the little prince was dropping off to sleep, I picked him up in my arms and walked on. I was deeply moved. It seemed to me that I was carrying something valuable and fragile. He felt like the most delicate thing on Earth. In the moonlight I looked at his pale forehead, his closed eyes, the locks of his hair that trembled in the wind, and I said to myself, 'What I see here is just his shell. The important bit is invisible.'

As his lips parted into a sleepy half-smile, I realized that what moved me so deeply about this little prince was his loyalty to his flower – the image of the rose seemed to glow inside him like a flame, even when he was asleep. And he felt even more fragile. One has to always protect a lamp from the wind.

I continued walking, and it was daybreak when I discovered the well.

CHAPTER 25

'People,' said the little prince, 'hop into express trains without knowing where they really want to go. They stumble about in circles, and get frustrated.'

He added. 'It is not worth all the trouble.'

The well that we found was not like the other wells of the Sahara which are holes dug in the sand. This one on the other hand looked like a village well. But there was no village and I thought I was dreaming.

'That's strange,' I said to the little prince. 'The pulley, the bucket, the rope – it's all there.'

He laughed, held the rope, and set the pulley to work. The pulley creaked, like a rusty weather vane, which had lain untouched by the wind for a long time.

'Did you hear?' said the little prince. 'The well is now awake, and it is singing.'

I did not want him to feel exhausted. 'Let me do it,' I said. 'This is too heavy for you.'

I hoisted the bucket slowly to the edge of the well and set it there. The song of the pulley was still in my ears, and I could see the trembling reflection of the sun in the water.

'I am thirsty,' said the little prince. 'Could I have a drink?'

And I understood what he had been looking for!

I lifted the bucket to his mouth. He drank, but his eyes were closed. It was beautiful. This water was indeed more than simple nourishment. Its sweetness was born of our long walk under the stars, the song of the pulley and my efforts through the night. It felt warm, like a present. When I was a little boy, the lights on the Christmas tree, the music of Midnight Mass, the tender smiling faces, made up for the eagerness of receiving gifts on the morning of Christmas.

'People on this planet,' said the little prince, 'grow five thousand roses in the same garden and yet do not find what they are looking for.'

'They do not,' I replied.

'Still, what they are looking for could be found in one single rose, or in a little water.'

'That is true,' I said.

And the little prince added, 'But the eyes are blind. One must see with the heart.'

Now that I had drunk the water, I breathed easily. At sunrise the sand takes on the colour of honey. And this colour made me happy. But what was it that made my heart so heavy with sorrow?

'You must keep your promise,' said the little prince softly, as he sat down beside me once more.

'What promise?'

'The muzzle for my sheep! I have to look after my flower.'

I took my sketches out of my pocket. The little prince looked through them, and laughed, 'These baobabs look like cabbages.'

'Oh!' And to think I had been so proud of my baobabs!

'Your fox's ears are too long and look like horns.'

He laughed again.

'That's not fair, little prince,' I said. 'All I have ever drawn is a boa constrictor with an elephant inside it.'

'Oh, but that's okay,' he said, 'children understand.'

I made a pencil sketch of a muzzle. I was a bit nervous handing it to him.

'You must understand, I do not know your plans,' I said.

But he did not answer. He said instead, 'You know my descent to Earth … tomorrow is the anniversary.'

Then, after a pause, he said, 'I landed close to this spot.'

And he blushed.

Once again, not knowing why, I felt a strange sadness.

But a question came to me, 'Then it wasn't an accident that on the morning when I first met you, a week ago, you were wandering by yourself, a thousand miles from civilization? You were trying to get back to the place where you had landed?'

The little prince blushed again.

And I added, with some uncertainty:

'And the reason is the anniversary?'

He blushed once more. He didn't usually answer questions, but when one blushes does that not mean they agree?

'I'm concerned,' I said to him.

But he stopped me. 'You must work now. Return to your engine. I'll wait for you here. Come back tomorrow night.'

I was still not comforted. I remembered the fox. Once tamed, you are in danger of being unhappy …

CHAPTER 26

Alongside the well stood a dilapidated old stone wall. The next night when I returned, I saw from a distance that my little prince was sitting on top of the wall with his feet dangling. And I heard him say, 'You don't remember. This is not the exact spot.'

Someone must have answered him, for he said, 'It is! It is the right day, but the wrong place.'

I continued moving towards the wall. I could not see or hear anyone. But the little prince replied once again, '... Exactly. You will see my footprints in the sand. You only have to wait. I will be there tonight.'

I was only twenty metres from the wall, and I still saw nothing.

After some time the little prince spoke again, 'Is your venom powerful? You are sure I'll not suffer too long?'

I stopped in my tracks, my heart beating fast; but I didn't quite understand.

'Now go away,' said the little prince. 'I want to get off the wall.'

I looked to the foot of the wall and flinched. There before me, facing the little prince, was one of those yellow snakes that could kill in less than thirty seconds. I moved forward even as I was digging in my pocket to

get my revolver out. But at the sounds I made, the snake slipped away quickly and disappeared between the rocks like a stream fading into the sand. I reached the wall just in time to catch my prince; his face was so very pale.

'What is going on?' I demanded. 'You've started talking to snakes?'

I loosened the golden muffler that he always had on. I rubbed his temples, and gave him some water to drink. And I held back from asking him any more questions. He looked at me gravely, and wrapped his arms around my neck. I felt his heart quivering like that of a dying bird.

'I am glad that you have figured out what was wrong with your engine,' he said.

'Now you can go home ...'

'But how did you know?'

That is what I was coming to tell him, that I had been successful in repairing the engine.

He gave me no answer, but said, 'I am going back home too … today.'

Then he added, rather sadly, 'It is much farther … much more difficult.'

I could sense that something incredible was about to happen. I held him like a child; and yet it seemed that he was falling fast into an abyss and there was no way to stop him.

He looked very serious, and had a faraway gaze.

'I have your sheep. I've got the sheep's box. And I have the muzzle.'

He gave me a sad smile.

I waited a long time. It seemed he was slowly recovering.

'My little man,' I said to him, 'you were afraid.'

There was no doubt that he was. But he let out a gentle laugh.

'I will be much more afraid tonight.'

Once again I felt myself gripped by a foreboding. I knew that I could not bear the thought of never hearing his laughter again. It was like a spring of fresh water.

'Little man,' I said, 'I want to hear your laugh again.'

But he said to me, 'Tonight it will be a year … my star will be exactly over the place where I landed last year.'

'Little man,' I said, 'tell me this is all a bad dream, the snake and the star.'

But he gave me no reply. 'The things that matter,' he repeated, 'are invisible.'

'Yes, I know …'

'Like it is with the flower. If you love a flower that lives on a star, it is wonderful to look up at the night sky. There is a flower on every star.'

'Yes, that's true …'

'It is like with the water. The drink of water you gave me was like music, because of the pulley, the rope … you remember … how good it was.'

'Yes, I remember.'

'At night you will look at the stars. It is difficult to tell you which one my planet is … it is too small. It is a good thing really. My star will be one among many. You will love watching them all … they will all be your friends. And, besides, I am going to give you a present.'

He laughed again.

'Ah, my little prince! How I love to hear your laugh!'

'That there is my present … just that … it will be like when we drank the water …'

'What are you saying?'

'People have their stars,' he answered, 'but they are not all the same. For travellers, the stars are guides. For others, they are simply little lights in the sky. For scientists, they are trouble. For my businessman, they were wealth. But the stars are silent. You … you alone … will have special stars.'

'What do you mean?'

'When you look at the starry sky, and as I will live on one of those stars, and I'll be laughing on one of those stars, it will seem to you that all the stars are laughing. You will have stars that can laugh!'

Saying this, he laughed again.

'And when you start to feel better, you will be happy that you knew me. You will always be a friend to me. You will want to laugh with me. And sometimes you will open your window and laugh. And your friends, surprised to see you laughing at the sky, will think you are mad! You will say to them, "Yes, the stars always make me laugh!" What a mischievous trick I would've played on you.'

And he laughed again.

'It will be as if I've given you little laughing bells instead of stars.'

He laughed once more. Then he quickly became serious, 'Tonight ... you know ... you shouldn't come.'

'I'm not leaving you,' I said.

'I will look distressed, like I was dying. That is how it will be. Do not come to see that. It is not worth the trouble.'

'I shall not abandon you.' But he was worried.

'I'm also trying to say ... it's because of the snake. It must not bite you. Snakes can be malicious creatures. Sometimes they bite just for fun.'

'I will not leave you.'

But a thought reassured him: 'They do not have enough venom to bite a second time.'

That night I did not hear or see him leave. When I caught up with him he was walking with determination, his steps quick and firm. 'Oh, you are here!' he said when he saw me.

And he took my hand. But he was still worried. 'Why did you come? You will suffer. I will look as if I was dead, but I won't be.'

I said nothing.

'You must understand … it is too far. I cannot carry this heavy body with me.'

I said nothing.

'It will be like an old abandoned skin. Old skins are not sad.'

I said nothing.

He was a little demoralized. But he tried one more time:

'You know, it will be very nice. I will look at the stars too. All the stars will be like wells with a rusty pulley. All the stars will pour fresh water for me to drink.'

I said nothing.

'It will really be delightful! You will have five hundred million little bells, and I will have five hundred million wells.'

Then he fell silent, because he had started to weep.

*

'Here we are. Let me now go on by myself.'

And he sat down, because he was afraid. Then he said, 'You know … my flower … she is my responsibility! And she is so delicate! She only has four thorns to keep herself safe.'

I sat down too, because I couldn't stand any longer.

'There … that is all …'

He hesitated a little, and then he got up. He took one step. I stayed frozen to the spot.

I saw a flash of yellow near his ankle. He remained unmoving for an second.

He didn't make any sound. He dropped gently like a tree. There was not even a thud as he fell on the sand.

CHAPTER 27

Six years have gone by. I have never told this story to anyone. My friends were thrilled to see me alive. I was sad, but I told them it was from fatigue.

Although I'm still sad, I feel a little soothed. I know the little prince is back on his planet, because the next morning I found his body gone. His was a light body … I love listening to the stars at night. It's like listening to five hundred million little bells.

But the strange thing is that I forgot to draw the leather strap on the sheep's muzzle for the little prince. He will never have been able to fasten it on his sheep. I wonder what happened on his planet. Did the sheep eat the flower?

But sometimes I say to myself: certainly not! The little prince covers the flower with the glass dome every night, and he watches over the sheep closely. Then I feel happy and the stars seem to giggle softly.

But at other times I imagine: during a moment of absentmindedness, he may have forgotten the glass dome, or the sheep escaped without his knowledge. That's when the little bells turn into tears!

*

Here, then, is the great mystery. For all those who love the little prince, like me, nothing in the universe can be the same if somewhere a sheep has eaten or not eaten a rose.

Look up at the sky. Ask yourselves: has the sheep eaten the flower? And you will see how everything changes.

And no grown-up will ever understand how important that is!

This, to me, is the most pleasing and the most woeful landscape in the world. It is the same as that on the preceding page, but I have drawn it again for you. It was here that the little prince appeared on Earth, and it was here that he disappeared.

Look at it carefully so that you will recognize it in case you travel someday to the African desert. And, if you should come upon this very spot, please do not hurry away. Wait a little under the star. Then, if you see a little boy with golden hair, who laughs and refuses to answer your questions, you will know who he is. If this should happen, please comfort me. Send me word that he has returned.